The River People

by Liz Kellebrew

UNSOLICITED PRESS
PORTLAND, OREGON

Kellebrew layers historical accounts, stories, and personal reflection in prose that courses with the assuredness of a river through time and perspectives, resulting in a lyrical and engaging account of family in the mid-19th century Pacific Northwest.

—Gail Folkins, author of *Light in the Trees*

The delicate construction of *The River People* makes me love it all the more—a kaleidoscopic portrait of Western Expansion, it is at once intimate and interrogating.

—Sarah C. Townsend, author of *Setting the Wire: A Memoir of Postpartum Psychosis*

Reading Liz Kellebrew's *The River People* is like taking a ride down the river itself. Sometimes gentle and other times roaring, its lyricism and mixed forms carry your heart through the flow of time. Run, don't walk, for your copy now!

—Sarah Cannon, author of *The Shame of Losing*

For information contact:
Unsolicited Press
Portland, Oregon
www.unsolicitedpress.com
orders@unsolicitedpress.com
619-354-8005

Interior Book Designer: Kathryn Gerhardt
Cover Designers: Kathryn Gerhardt
Editor: Summer Stewart

ISBN: 978-1-963115-27-7

*To my family, my friends,
and my fellow travelers on the river of life*

Autumn's tint was on the leaf.
The waning day was drawing near.
There was a river flowing by clear
And bright fresh from distant mountains'
Ancient glacial field,
Flowing on and on to the stiller waters of
The broader valley.

Flow thou river, flow thou on.
Thy soft evening breeze forever gone,
Thy presence now becomes aeon.

James Meikle

1852: MARILLA

When the river takes you, you will know. That's why my brother Henry didn't make a sound. One moment he was fording the wagon across the river, next he was yanked down under, at the mercy of the current made mighty by autumn rain.

Rivers have no mercy. This is what the West has taught me.

My name is Marilla Washburn. I am twelve years old. A woman now, or so I am told. My parents' oldest living child.

Here at Fort Vancouver, the sky is always gray and weeping, matching my mother's tears. I cry too. I cannot lie. There is nothing here for us but cholera and death, or suffering, if we survive.

This journey has taken us over two thousand miles, and now we are in a place that is nothing like home. It is all mud, flooding, and rain. Dark clouds and deep forests that crowd around you, choking out life. We are shriveled and wasting; I can count all my bones. The food at the fort is bland and watery, but I must eat it anyway. It is the only thing keeping me alive.

When you cross the prairie, it seems there is nothing but sky. Bright white-blue sky, darker blue at the edges, with the sun hot above. It's impossible to get lost here. The ruts from all the wagons that have gone before are deep and wide, worn to a brown like a buffalo's hide.

The year Marilla and her family came west, as many as 6,000 people and their animals walked the same route over a period of six months. Everyone walking in the tracks of those who'd come before. Everyone needing water for life.

They had to drink from the same source as their livestock. Their water was often contaminated with animal and human waste, rife with cholera bacteria.

Home on the Oregon Trail was a box with a tent on top, pulled by oxen, rolling on wooden wheels. You lived that way for two thousand miles between your old home in the east and your new home out west, a home that you would have to build for yourself out of the trees and the land.

Covered wagons could travel up to twenty miles per day, depending on the weather. Despite her nineteenth-century mode of transportation, Marilla moved farther during her lifetime than I have during mine.

The truth: I'm afraid to leave what I know.

There are ruts from the Oregon Trail so deep you can see them still. Twin lines where no grass grows. An unhealed wound on the land, with buried bones to mark the way.

A few years of travel, and ruts endure for 150 years. A few decades of burning coal, and even the moths change color to blend into their newly sooty surroundings. A few years of driving cars across a grated bridge in Hood Canal, and tire particles poison scores of salmon. A couple big bombs were built to end one war and spent plutonium rods leak into the soil for millennia.

Eventually, the earth reclaims her own. Retribution is swifter than you think.

...a great wave of excitement, the Western fever, swept over all that part of the country. Nearly everybody was talking about the Willamette Valley, the Puget Sound country, or California. Father decided to go to Oregon. He made a contract to bring four families across the plains, he to furnish wagons, teams and drivers for a stipulated amount.

We started out with five wagons. Father brought out some blooded mares. One of them was a fine Morgan mare. Two of our wagons were drawn by horses and the other three by oxen.

Marilla Washburn

She gathers camas roots in her skirts. Bonnet swinging from her neck. She is brown as the earth, as the world.

Most of the time we walked barefoot. We went ahead of the wagons so we wouldn't choke on their dust. We stubbed our toes on rocks and had to keep a sharp eye out for rattlesnakes and cacti.

But when we rode the horses, we flew like birds in the wind. The prairie dust below us distant as clouds.

One thing true about this universe: all living things must eat. Sometimes, they get to choose what they eat. Sage hens and jackrabbits were readily available along the Oregon Trail, but Marilla and her siblings hated them. They preferred antelope and buffalo.

The buffalo would come on a cloud of dust with a noise like thunder. Like ocean waves, Marilla said, when she was older and had lived by the Pacific. The buffalo ran slowly, but as one, an unyielding herd of massive creatures running to the river to drink. Wagon trains had to divide themselves to let the buffalo through.

It was easy, then, to think that the buffalo would always multiply. Easy to think there would always be enough.

This land rolls on, flat plains unspooling like cloth ripped open by the slow burn of a river, punctured by the crucifix of an ancient tree.

We hear the buffalo before we see them. They are a sound like the crashing of ocean waves. We see their great dust billow up from the horizon and I feel an animal fear in my belly, a knowing of death in my ribs. My heart beats fast as we pull the team to a halt.

The buffalo do not stop for anything, or so we have heard. But as we wait under the cover of our wagon, the earth seizing and quaking in fits, the buffalo part around us, running on. Their great hairy bodies stink of musk and manure, their powerful shoulders rolling on and on like the endless plain.

We used to see a cloud of dust rising, and Father would call out to get ready to divide the train. Soon we would hear a low roar, like the sound of surf, and then we would see a big herd of shaggy-haired buffaloes, their heads held low, running at a slow lumbering trot to the river to drink. They wouldn't stop for anything, so we gave them the right of way. Several times we had to divide our train to let them through. We ate buffalo meat and antelope. Some of the families ate sage hens and jackrabbits, but we kids didn't like them and would go hungry before we would eat them.

Marilla Washburn

Stand in an open plain where the rim of the skydome, entirely unnotched by so much as a hill, entirely encircles you, especially at sunrise or sunset, try to see the end of things and you can't. Earth seems to reach to never, never, and you almost forget there is any under your feet; in fact, you seem to be in suspension. Then, startled, you are again conscious of the ground beneath you.

Really, vastness is even more impressed upon you than in the company of stupendous heights. Loneliness is more apt to seize you, and you are imprisoned, for there is no landmark where you may go. With no hills and mountains to beckon you, you essay to keep on direction, but when will somewhere come in sight?

Walter Meikle

This country feels like forever. Grassy plains, clouds, sun, sometimes rain. The furry heads of dandelions gone to the wind. I do not remember the way the world was before: no churches, no cities, no clapboard houses listing gray along the horse-muddied streets. No wells, no privies. No amber fields of grain.

Just the flat wide rivers and the tall grass, the rabbits in the weeds. The buffalo on a thousand hills. The lusty shrieks of coyote—every night when we try to sleep, they come closer.

We are getting closer to our destination. The destiny of a nation: the West.

MANIFEST DESTINY: AN INTERROGATION

And we are now men, and must accept in the highest mind that same transcendent destiny; ...let us advance on Chaos and the Dark.

Emerson

We men must move forward without delay, for our one transcendent destiny is to subdue the earth and its creatures, making manifest the kingdom of our inner light.

Order we bring to the mutinous forests, whose cedars and firs we will fell to build homes and mills. Light we bring to the dark and overgrown valleys, whose lush river plains we will seed with potatoes and apple trees.

Instead of cougar and bear, we bring cattle and horses to a thousand hills, acres and acres of savage land converted to farms and logging camps, houses and towns.

The day will come when this land will all be ours, those Indigenous nations nothing more than a smallpox memory. Wild beasts that devour will become as extinct as medieval demons. No man-eaters prowling these woods.

The cities and mills will stretch on as far as the eye can see. The smoke of our descendants' doings shall likewise rise. The roads and highways will be filled with goods and movement, the heat of exchange melting gold into circuits that do not decay.

And the light, our glorious light! will shine on forevermore, lighting the night until there is no more darkness, no more predators lurking in the shadows or heathen stars winking in the night. All of our works will be made manifest for the world to see, for God Himself to see and say that we are good.

Because we *are* good… aren't we?

My people have a saying about that time. I will try to translate it here: "It was the winter of broken hearts."

1852–1854: MARILLA

Rushing water. Fording the currents. Wagon and oxen, following the rest. Rain and thunder, she's soaked to the bone. But her brother has it the worst, in the water with Father, coaxing the animals across.

The wagon lurches. Father's outside yelling orders to Henry but something's wrong. Henry's screaming, then he's gone.

Marilla tears open the wagon flaps, receives a mouthful of sky. Father's strangely silent, they've stopped halfway across. The river churns, the wagon lists, they're going to be tipped over and carried away and Mother cries out loud and Father whips the oxen and they somehow ford the river but Henry's gone, sucked down into the muddy waters. Snake River has swallowed him whole.

They never find his body.

Dark beneath black basaltic walls,
Through fossil beds,
The sunlight of other days
And other years sealed
In night's stone sepulcher.

Where primeval forests reached down to
The shoreline in unbroken unison
Protecting each other in storms
In the realm of the unknown one by one.

James Meikle

On the worst days, when I'm weak from another bout of cholera, drenched to the bone, and hungry but unable to eat, I think to myself, this land was not meant for people. We are not meant to be here.

Cholera is a *she*. She reduces men to begging for their mothers, pants around their ankles, dying naked as the day they were born. The cramps come like a woman's labor, curling you up into a ball as you excrete your life into the recesses of the earth.

Two hours later, you are dead. Then it is a woman who labors to wash the soil off your body, a woman who combs your hair and changes your clothes, who wipes the filth out of your secret places and prepares you for the cleanliness of heaven, who washes off your humanity before you enter the presence of the most high God.

A man says a prayer over your corpse. Your possessions are distributed among the living. You are buried in the dark brown soil of the earth, a cross nailed above your head. Someone writes your mother a letter. You are full of gas and disease.

The next day, the wagon train moves on without you. Another man rides your horse.

A day later, you are crawling with earthworms and beetles.

On the third day, your spirit takes flight.

The wagon train moves on without you. Cholera hikes up her skirts, walks in their tracks.

*There were 170 men, women and children. Captain Berry…
took the mountain fever and could no longer serve as captain, so
my father was elected captain. Just after the Fourth of July, some
of the members of our train took smallpox, and four died of it.*

*Two days before we came to Chimney Rock, the cholera struck
us. Seven died in our train that night and four the next day. A
young man in our wagon train named Hyde went out as a guard
for the stock that night. When he left after supper, he seemed
perfectly well. When the guard was changed at midnight, Mr.
Wood brought his body back to the train. He had been taken with
severe cramps and died within two hours.*

*My brother and I both took the cholera. Mother gave us all
the hot whiskey she could pour down us and put flannel cloths
soaked in whiskey, as hot as we could bear them, on our stomachs.
This cured us. Father was a veterinary surgeon. He had brought a
lot of medicine for horses and cattle and also the family medicine
chest. My mother was a good practical nurse; in fact she had to be
to raise fourteen children.*

Marilla Washburn

Too many people had died, and now the remaining souls only wanted to make sure their children could eat. Exploration became a lost cause. The maps of the known world shrank.

When they planted their gardens, they plowed rigid, parallel paths. They built their homes like fortresses: boxed-in squares, sharp angles, blockades on the landscape.

They didn't know that there is more than one way to go West.

It was autumn. He was leading the livestock across the river, his horse warm beneath him, the chill rainwater dripping down the brim of his hat. With the reins wrapped tight around his fist, he began to cross.

"Whoa, girl, whoa." He patted his horse's neck as she sidestepped into the river. Spooked by the rapids, she whinnied loud and sharp, kicked up water cold as ice. The river soaked into his clothes and chilled him. He tried to steady her, but she bucked.

He fell into the wild river. Heard his father calling his name. His horse reared above him as he groped for the reins. One powerful hoof hit his head. The world went silent and gray.

I was sick with fever in the back of the wagon, Mother caressing my head. We saw the river take him, Henry my brother, my mother's son, and yank him downstream like an autumn leaf.

It's my fault she couldn't save him, couldn't be there to reach out and take his hand. The river was so cold. It must have killed him within minutes.

Tides and rivers rise with frequency and force in western Washington. Many pioneers on the Oregon Trail rafted down the Columbia River from The Dalles for the final leg of their journey, arriving at Fort Vancouver. The garden at the fort was planted on the riverbank, facing south. It flooded often during the winter. And after a good hard rain, the river's currents could sweep you clean away.

It was treacherous traveling in the autumn when Marilla and her family arrived. They would have had to choose between rafting the cold and wild Columbia, or traveling over the mountain pass where wagon axles and horse's legs often broke, and sudden snowfall could trap travelers, starving them out.

They took the Columbia River route to Fort Vancouver. At the fort, English, French, Cree, Hawaiian, and other native languages were spoken, but Chinook jargon was the common trading language.

The eventual state motto of Washington, "Alki," is a Chinook word. The meaning roughly translates to "Bye and bye," implying the passage of time and the reunion of separated friends. A popular hymn of that era, "In the Sweet Bye and Bye," describes reuniting with lost loved ones in heaven. Separated from friends and relatives by thousands of miles, in a time when travel was limited to ships, horses and wagons, and one's own two feet, the most a new migrant could hope for was a reunion in the afterlife.

Winter is coming, and the family presses on. West and then west. There is nowhere else to go.

When we got to The Dalles, Father sold his blooded mares and his stock to the government. In those days there was a fort at The Dalles. Father left his five wagons there, intending to go back and get them later but he never went back. We went from The Dalles to the Cascades on a flatboat. There we caught a small steamer for Vancouver.

Marilla Washburn

To get back to Vancouver was a pleasure, and to look at clear rivers and green hills and breathe the fresh air gave a lift to the spirit. I had always been moved at the sight of the great mountains of this Northwest and to behold their magnitude and majesty. When one is close to them, they cut off a great section of the sky and loom large in their vastness.

Walter Meikle

Clouds, rain. Clouds, rain. Weeks and weeks of the same. The river by the fort creeps over its banks and floods the fields where the fort grows its food.

I don't cry as often anymore. I am doing laundry and cooking and other things that need doing. Mother is suffering from sickness of the heart.

This is how the river broke her heart: it made promises it couldn't keep, talking all night while we tried to sleep. Relentless, exhausting, it churned. Eroding the banks, rushing over the backs of salmon, the river ran mad, a slick throbbing wound on the face of the earth.

My most vivid recollection of that first winter... is of the weeping skies and of Mother and me also weeping. I was homesick for my schoolmates..., and I thought I would die.

Marilla Washburn

It rains so much where I live that I've come to expect it. It's the sunny weather that surprises me.

Winter in western Washington is a wet cold, the kind of cold that makes you long for a warm fire and dry socks. Seventy-three inches of rain falls on average each year, with the majority falling from November to February. Condensation becomes a way of life, a filter through which you see the world: through fogged bus windows, rain-beaded kitchen windows, streaked eyeglasses, drenched eyelashes.

Walking in Seattle, I learned that eyebrows can only hold so much water. At a certain point, they overflow, rain filling the pockets of your eyelids and clouding your vision.

The world seen through a raindrop is ovoid and bright. Too bright, like sun on snow, like the sun glaring off a skyscraper's edge. Even under a sky of dark gray clouds, raindrops make you see light. The light follows wherever you look. The pooling rainwater in the gutters reflects color and sky. Gray becomes silver and stunning white. The bridal sheen of winter.

Marilla would be a bride at fifteen. Story of woman, of the world. It was her destiny to bear children, cook, and clean. Her first winter in Washington State, the days were dark, the world unkind. She'd barely survived cholera. Her brother had died. She knew no one in her new home. Her mother couldn't stop crying. Neither could the sky.

She wept, too. She couldn't help it. She'd seen so much death along the way, and there in the middle of nowhere the dark winter days held no promise. She thought she would die. This was a surprisingly rational thought. So crying was a rational response, there in a cold bunk at a muddy fort among strangers where the rain fell so hard the river overflowed its banks. No matter how much the rain fed the river, the river still wanted more. Its churning brown mouth devoured the fort's garden, making both food and travel impossible.

Stuck at the fort! Where cholera had followed myriad travelers, where no one was safe from disease or hunger or the cold. Where homesickness was an ache in your gut. A longing for friends you once knew, for family you could count on, for a warm fire and dry roof and a brother not dead.

In Washington, most of the days in fall and winter are dark. The rain can be oppressive, a weighted blanket, like sleep paralysis. You want to move but you can't, some watery weight is pinning you down, you wake to more dark and gray and think, this will never end, but then it does. One day it is different. One day is just a few minutes longer, one day there is a thirty-minute sunbreak. One day the rain stops and the odor of geosmin rises from the earth. The chickadees sing and the river returns to its own bed. The smelt return, sating hunger.

The Pacific Northwest may have one of the rainiest winters in the country, but it also has one of the longest springs.

We traveled the river to come to the fort. But Mother and I couldn't make ourselves look at the water. We couldn't help but think of poor Henry, his body rotting away in pieces among the rocks upstream.

My brother, in the bellies of the fish. He should have been called Jonah.

He wasn't in the habit of looking for bodies as he paddled down the river, but it was the smell that caught him first. The sweet bitter stink of death, a smell he knew from butchering pigs at the farm, a smell he tried to avoid.

Then he saw it: a slack, blue body swathed in muddy rags, bumping gently against the old snag hanging over the river bend. The build was slight and short; some mother's son, no doubt, although by now his facial features were well worn away.

Llewellyn put his canoe onto shore. He lifted the body out by the shoulders of its cotton shirt; the weave still held, even as the edges of the flesh sloughed away like spilled jelly.

The stench was unbearable.

He laid the body on the riverbank. Sewn inside the boy's coat he found a name tag inscribed with indelible ink. *Henry Washburn.*

With his knife, he cut off the tag. He turned Henry's pockets inside out. A tiny silver horseshoe shone bright against the dark river soil. He picked it up.

The stench was unbearable, but all too familiar. Lord knows how many boys he would've buried if he'd stayed home for the war. As it was, he barely had the will to bury this one.

He piled the body high with a cairn of river stones. He went away from there.

I want to climb inside a tree the way the rain does. Surging through whiskery roots, swelling up sapwood rings into branches and leaves, exhaling semaphore signals from terrene into the cosmos.

When my body fades, I will give myself back to the earth, feeding the pine tree that sang at my birth.

I want you to bury me in the rain when I die. Don't wait too long. Carry me out while my body's still warm, steam rising off my skin to meet the everlasting sky.

My brother, Henry, just older than I, who was 14, was a fine horseman and expert swimmer. When we reached the Snake River, Father told Henry to take the stock across where they could get better pasture.

The horse Henry rode became frightened in the swift water and began flaunting around and got into deep water. When my brother tried to get him back into shallower water, he reared up, threw Henry off his back and kicked him in the head.

We stayed there two days searching for my brother's body.

Henry drowned just above Salmon Falls. Mother wrote a notice and fastened it to a board beside the road asking anyone who found Henry's body to bury it and notify her.

The next spring, we got a letter from a man named Llewellyn who had settled above Salem. He said he had found Henry's body and buried it. He sent Mother the things he had found in Henry's pockets.

Just before leaving Chicago, a chum of Henry's had given him a small horseshoe for good luck. Before we left home, Mother wrote our names in indelible ink on strong pieces of cloth and sewed them inside our clothes. Mr. Llewellyn cut from Henry's jacket the label with his name on it, and the little good luck horseshoe, and sent them to Mother.

Marilla Washburn

Mrs. Bush shows us how to make jam with Oregon grapes. Oregon grapes are small and sour. They don't taste good without sweetener. Now that we've picked plenty of fruit, it goes into a kettle on the woodstove, with some sugar and a bit of water. I stir it and the grapes pop as the mixture boils down.

Mrs. Bush tells us we should eat Oregon grapes so we don't get scurvy. You can drink fir needle tea instead, but that doesn't taste nearly as good.

Mother pours cornbread batter into the cast iron and puts it in the stove. The jam is almost reduced by half now. I've been stirring so long my arms are sore. Mrs. Bush sings as she churns the butter.

I smell the cornbread baking as the jam thickens and coats the back of the spoon. We let the jam cool on the table, pat fresh butter lumps onto the knob. Father and Mr. Bush are smoking river salmon outside over a fire. Their laughter sounds like home.

When Mother cuts the cornbread, its steam fogs the knife. We are all so eager to taste it that we forget to say grace, but it's alright. The melted butter on the crumbling bread, warm jam tart on the tongue, and the pink salmon flaking against the roof of my mouth is grace enough.

The days fly. We fell logs, build houses. Plow fields for next spring's crops. Catch fish in the Cowlitz River, chop firewood, make soap from fat and ashes.

When the smelt run in the month of February, we dip a net in the river and come up with enough to eat for days. We smoke them like the Cowlitz people do. One of my favorite treats.

A feeling of sadness, the browning leaves of the salmonberry,

The crickets speaking in sound of pathos, the closing of the season,

The going with an aunt to visit another aunt and uncle far back in the woods,

The lonely feeling that came over me as soon as I saw the little open patch

in miles of endless forest,

The echo of the little lath hammer on the forest wall as I pounded on the porch

to drive away the loneliness.

The creak of the latchstring doors, which lingered down the years,

The deathly hopeless stillness, not a sound,

The very elements ceased to breathe.

The great stub crashed to earth.

The twisted sagging gate fell across the trail.

A few pickets departing from its rotted frame slid farther down the hill.

James Meikle

It is good to be in this log cabin we built with our own hands, the fireplace and chimney of river rocks and clay, moss and mud we children placed in the chinks between the logs where now the rain and wind sneak in. We may not have glass windows or wooden floors. But I find I am alright with that. There is more to life than fine things, I think, reading by the firelight. Two years ago we thought we'd die. Isn't this enough?

There is a word for people with movable homes. *Vagrant.* The connotation is derogatory. It is the same with the word *homeless.* In this country, we spit the word out as though the poor had done something purposeful to opt out of more permanent homes. As if there is something wrong with unhoused people and not with the system that decides who is or isn't worthy of a dwelling with solid walls.

It used to be a lot easier to build your own house with materials found at hand. Trees, for instance. When Marilla and her family came to Washington, some people hollowed out large stumps and put a shake roof on top, living in the tree until they could build a log cabin. Some Native Americans in the area built longhouses on stilts to avoid flooding when tides or rivers rose.

Today, we are just as ingenious at creating places to shelter. But some of us are punished for it.

Most unpoetical rounding to our three thousand miles of staging in these ten weeks of travel, was this ride through Washington. The road was rough beyond description; during the winter rains it is just impassable, and is abandoned; for miles it is… simply a path cut through the dense forest….

But the majestic beauty of the fir and cedar forests, through which we rode almost continuously for the day and a half that road stretched out, was compensation for much discomfort. These are the finest forests we have yet met….

Washington Territory must have more timber and ferns and blackberries and snakes to the square mile than any other State or Territory of the Union. We occasionally struck a narrow prairie… but for the most part it was a continuous ride through forests, so high and thick that the sun could not reach the road, so unpeopled and untouched, that the very spirit of Solitude reigned supreme, and made us feel its presence as never upon Ocean or Plain.

Samuel Bowles

I feel that moving to Washington Territory has changed me completely. I watched my brother die, and I almost died myself. I used to think I could never be happy here, but since then I have learned to love this place. The dark green firs, named for the botanist David Douglas. The Cowlitz and Chehalis people who still live near their namesake rivers, paddling their long canoes. I learned to speak some of their jargon at Fort Vancouver, so Mother sends me down to the river to trade eggs and milk for other things we need. Salt and vanilla, calico and thread.

When Father is working the fields, I ride his horse and run errands for him. Getting the mail from the boat, delivering messages to the neighbors, things like that. Back in Illinois, young ladies my age would never be allowed to go riding alone like this. But it is perfectly safe here, and there is no such thing as high society, so I'm not required to be proper. This is Freeport, and here I am free, this river and forest my home.

The river swells with rain and swallows the land. It fills the fields and makes new lakes among the reeds and tall grass. It seeps up from the earth, taking the form of every imprint in the mud: our shoes, the horses' hooves, the prints of deer, coyote, and rabbit.

At Fort Vancouver, the Chinook told stories of our sisters and brothers the salmon and ravens. It sounded strange to me then. But here by the river with the evergreen trees, I am with the animals every day. I hear ravens call at dusk and dawn. I go fishing and watch the salmon swim upstream. The coyotes sing us to sleep every night, prompting Father to reinforce the chicken coop. Deer graze in the morning hours, wreathed in fog at the edge of the cabin clearing.

One night I went to the outhouse and stopped to admire the moon. Suddenly, three deer ran out of the woods. Five coyotes followed, silent and swift as thieves.

How quiet nature is when it is time to kill.

1842–1854: JOHN

I know what it is to have freedom mean more than the bread
you eat. What it is to give your all when you don't have nothing
to start with. To know you might never get anything back.

Well I remember those days in old Cookstown, where Father moved the family when the farm was no longer enough to feed us. He opened a textile mill there on the Ballinderry, one more mill among many others, and there at the ripe old age of twelve I was put right to work. It was hot, fast, meaningless work, spooling wool onto spindles for the machines to dye and weave into rough gray blankets. My hands bled and my mind went numb, standing for hours on end doing nothing but changing spindles for those hulking machines.

The only comfort I could take was in the memories of the farm, of shearing and shepherding the sheep, whose damp wool was now spun into factory blankets and sold in faraway lands like America.

I liked to think about America, the things we heard about its distant shores. How there was no fighting between Oranges and Catholics because all beliefs were welcome there. How glistening cities had sprung up on its shores overnight. How the land teemed with plant, animal, and mineral riches there for the taking, if a man would put his sweat into it.

In the gray hours of the early morning and evening, as I walked to and from the factory, I caught sight of the old cross at Ardboe. It was nigh on a thousand years old, and I thought to myself how ancient this place was, how long we Irish had lived here, and how many years had gone by with nothing changed. Excepting the factories, which were a shite deal as far as I was concerned. My Da barely made enough to feed us, and I myself earned no wages working for him. Da said I was working for my room and board, and someday my efforts would pay off when he died and I inherited the place.

But drinking as much as he did, I could see only two paths in my future. Either he drank away all the profits and left me bankrupt, or he drank himself into an early grave and I was stuck with the miserable life he had chosen for himself, and no way out of my forced drudgery.

In the end I did what we Irish do best. I made a third way of my own choosing: I would go to America.

Da near beat me to death when I broke the news. Ma intervened, hugged me tight. Told me to leave and not look back.

I was sixteen years old.

Cast the bantling on the rocks,
Suckle him with the she-wolf's teat,
Wintered with the hawk and fox,
Power and speed be hands and feet.

Emerson

Liverpool didn't look too kindly on Irishmen, but it was here that the great ships left for the New World, and to pay my passage I still needed a job. I learned right quick to go by the surname Black, common enough for the English around those parts. I paid for room and board and slowly earned my fare by handling cargo for the ships, disguising my accent the best I could.

It took me longer to save for the trip than I'd like to admit, and all the while I considered I might never see my homeland again. But in the end, I decided it was for the best. That place was full of memories, few of them pleasant. The black eye from my old man a prime example. Da wouldn't be so bad if he weren't always in a bottle, but whiskey and Da were like salt and the sea. No one could change that.

It was cold as a dead fish and sleeting sideways when my ship shoved off from Liverpool. Myself and a few hundred other fine lads, making our way across the ocean to the New World.

Sometimes, when the wind isn't so bad, I stand on the deck for the sheer heck of it. I hold on to the railing and look down at the oily black of the sea, then up at the white of the sky. We're the only ship for miles and miles. No welcome lights on the horizon.

I hold my breath. Then I breathe. Each second takes me farther from home and closer to that new continent, a place I've only seen in dreams.

When I saw New York City all gold on the horizon, I thought this must be what heaven looked like. The immigration office on Ellis Island gave me another impression entirely.

I was grateful not to be sent home. If I ever showed my face in Cookstown again, I was sure my father would kill me out of sheer spite.

John didn't waste much time in New York before sailing to Oregon around Cape Horn. The voyage took several months. It cost more than traveling by ox or horse on the Oregon Trail, which was itself expensive. Sailing took less time than the six months required for the overland trail. But sailing around Cape Horn also took more time than sailing to Panama, crossing over land to the other side of the isthmus, and taking another ship from there. That cut sailing time in half, but it was far more dangerous.

However, John Black had the means to take the safer boat route around two continents. Yes, it was treacherous sailing around the tip of South America. But it was less dangerous than the rampant disease, hunger, and violence along the Oregon Trail, which at this point was crowded with greedy forty-niners on their way to California, gold lust in their sights.

Local legend says that where the path to California forked off from the Oregon Trail, there were two signs. One sign had the word "Oregon" written on it, and the other was painted with a picture of gold nuggets. The joke goes that the people who could read went to Oregon. Indeed, even in the early twenty-first century, Oregon boasted a literacy rate of 90%. California's was 77%.

The ships that sailed around Cape Horn were often overcrowded. Ship's captains squeezed on as many passengers as they could get away with. There were profits to be made.

The voyage around the cape was famously hair-raising. Currents and winds converged, oceans collided, ships were tossed and frequently wrecked on the rocks. Passengers fell overboard. Seasickness was rampant. But it was still safer than the Oregon Trail.

So it turned out that New York didn't look too kindly on the Irish, either. New world, same old problems. I and my fellow passengers are packed into this creaking tub like clams in a can, stinking in our own juices. Surrounded by an ocean's worth of water, but nary a bath for forty days. And we've got 140 more to go.

I've got too much time to think. To regret. That I couldn't take Ma and my brothers and sisters with me, away from the wrath of Da. Away from a future that's been chosen for them, practically carved in stone.

I write letters home, knowing full well that if anything happens to the ship, they may never get sent. I eat my daily ration slowly so as not to upset my stomach any more than the waves already have. I go out onto the deck and gaze at the western horizon until the salt wind stings my eyes.

One thing's for sure: I never look back.

I walk off the gangplank onto dry land for the first time in weeks. The sun is high and hot, so painfully bright that I dare not raise my eyes. My legs wobble as I walk along the docks, a feeling I remember from my previous Atlantic voyage.

The noises of Rio de Janeiro rise up to greet me: grizzled Portuguese sailors and swarthy locals barking in the Europeans' tongue, fishermen shouting friendly commands as they unload their catch, the bells of the mission chiming for prayers. Someone is playing a high-pitched flute, a series of minor notes that spiral in the smoke from cookfires and kettles in the market square.

Pretty women with jacaranda blossoms in their hair gather in groups at the fountain, drawing water and washing clothes. Their clothing is as multicolored as the fruits in the marketplace, shades of red and green and yellow so vibrant they shock the senses. And deep blues and purples like the first dark of an evening sky.

Man may possess the fire and drive to traverse the globe, but it is woman who makes him feel he's home.

Learning is the product of curiosity, a trait which is bred out of us as often as creativity is. Indeed, both curiosity and creativity are the natural state of humankind; learning, growth, and development as a biological species cannot evolve without those traits. To the restrictive binary of either/or, yes/no, the human in their best/natural state says *all* and *infinite* and *possible*. All possibilities are open to the inquiring mind and creative thought.

You have to spend some time in this place to know what it is about. To know who you are about, you must also know the place in which you live, so it is in your best interest to learn all you can about the living world around you. This self-education can of course be supplemented by book learning, but the sort of original inquiry this knowledge requires can only come from a keen sense of observation. How does the wind taste, for example; what do these trees smell of; which creature constructed that particular nest, which fungus sprouts that exact shade of brilliant pink?

Like Richard Feynman's atomic particle, every possible path leads the curious soul to exactly wherever they are meant to be, so that the final state of the explorer is the sum of all their experiences lived as one brilliant and candid life, which can only be achieved by doing the opposite of what most schools teach: by accepting without judgment, by avoiding the craven impulse to categorize and confine knowledge to hierarchically imposed domains. Instead, look. Listen. Taste. Touch. Breathe.

They say this is the worst part: going through the Strait. Ships and lives are lost here, where Pacific, Atlantic, and Antarctic oceans converge, carving that sharp geography that curls from the tip of South America.

The ocean is a slippery beast, a great dark placenta trailing the end of some vicious gorgon's birth. Just when I think I've grown accustomed to the pitch and yaw of the waves, we hit another squall and I learn all over again how to keep my biscuits down, or not. There's certainly no extra food to be spared for replacing the expelled contents of one's stomach.

We're all praying to our Maker. We're already on our knees.

Finally, we've made it to the Oregon coast. It's beautiful. Sheer rock cliffs plunge into the sea, the white crests of black waves breaking on golden boulders. Thick forests cover the tops of the cliffs like a giant's hair: spruce and Douglas fir, named by an early Pacific Northwest explorer, I am told. And western hemlocks, the ones with tops that curl over like question marks. Some of these with trunks so wide five men can't reach around it.

The crew discusses our final approach. We'll navigate a dangerous sandbar known as the Graveyard of the Pacific. Hundreds of ships have met their ends here. In this wild place with no markers either on land or at sea, the captain must rely on the skills of his navigators and trust that the maps he follows are still true. For there is one thing certain about the sea: she is always changing, and she is shifting the sands beneath her weight, and shaping the curves of new beaches and spits everywhere she goes.

A willful lass, the sea. We get along just fine, she and I. Maybe it's the independent streak we have in common, a bit of courage to go beyond what's expected, to dream the impossible dream. Sure, she's subject to the tides just like I am, pulled this way and that by the demands of the moon. But the whole time she's rearranging the coastline to her liking, throwing up driftwood here, sea kelp there, cultivating clams and castles.

In Ireland we had ancient fortresses perched on crags, surrounded by sea, where kings and queens and chieftains of old waged war and love. Hard to believe I am descended from such men as these, I of the lanky arms and too-big teeth. But then again maybe I am. Although I left my country behind, leaving a bad place in search of a better one, I've come to this wildest of outposts, this Astoria of which Irving writes. This place where a man can be free to worship God in his own way and live at peace with his neighbors, more than enough land at his disposal to make a living and provide for his family. I will make my own fortress of solitude and ingenuity, here at the edge of the world, and I will build my castle surrounded by trees, and grow fat and serene on the fruits of the land.

When the lightning stopped, the sun appeared and we evaporated. Cell by cell we rose into the sky and joined the cirrus clouds in a layer of high fog. We could see everything: the fires in the alpine forests, sagebrush plateaus and painted hills, the tide pools filled with barnacles and anemones.

We drank the rain until it spilled from our pores.

Senescent, the trees climb, up and away from the sea like windblown pilgrims. I've been around the coasts of both Americas, North and South, their continents vast and unknowable.

And there's the city, with all its colorful clapboard houses on the hill, John Jacob Astor's empire glowing like a rainbow in the afternoon sun. I feel a sense of longing for the home I'll soon make my own, so different from how I felt about the Old World.

Just as quickly, my excitement is replaced by grief for the family I've left behind. I'm on the other side of the world now. I'll never see them again.

We dock the ship and it's time to leave. Some of my fellow passengers take me to the tavern for drinks. I told myself I'd never be like Da, but this one night I get pickled on some white corn whiskey.

We take the bottle out behind the cannery and sit with the herring, their dead eyes shining under the bright full moon. We sing until dawn.

MANIFEST DESTINY: AN INTERROGATION

From a fort you get a trading post, and from a trading post you will get a city.

John Jacob Astor

The long arm and hand of the LORD will surely catch up to ye. Long live the man who cleaves unto His Word.

The rest of ye sinners, daughters of Eve whose stain of natural sin is upon you and your children forever and ever—it is up to us good Christian men to bring the Word and the hand of the LORD to guide you. Without us, your husbands and fathers, you would be as lost as the heathens that fill this land, as savage as the wild grizzly, who will tear out the throats of men when she has cubs. You wouldn't last a day out here without us, no—for the weakness of women is complemented by the strength of men, as you know and God hath ordained.

Let me ask you this—who would protect you, wife, and your young sons and daughters, if I were not here with my whip and gun? Spare the rod, spoil the child; spare the fist, spoil the wife. Better that I should discipline you than the savage beasts of night. Better that I should cause you some small harm now, that you should not go astray and find the mercy of the West dangling you by the neck from a rope and pole. Better that I should lead and guide you as the divinely appointed hand of God and rule over my house in a manner befitting the Kingdom of Heaven, for we are the Kingdom of Heaven made manifest on Earth, we are the chosen sons to settle and have dominion over this land. We are the ones whose destiny leads us into this wild West and we will make our kingdoms on this earth, yes, starting with our wives and sons and daughters, starting with our ox whip and pistol, starting with the embers of our hearth so carefully tended by our obedient wives, we will stoke this homely fire until its godly tongues of flame alight and spread all over this land.

God will not have his work made manifest by cowards.

Emerson

In the grand scheme of things, civilization is the anomaly, permanent habitation the aberration.

1854: JOHN

The steamboat carries me up the Columbia River smooth as a song. I take a flatboat the rest of the way up the Cowlitz. When I arrive in Freeport, there's a pretty girl on a horse waiting for the boat to come in.

I shoulder my pack and plod up the riverbank. She's trading something with the oarsman, oblivious to me.

Then my ankle rolls in the soft river sand, and I go down like a sack of potatoes. My face is on fire as I scramble to my feet but there's one point in my favor: she's no longer oblivious.

Before highways or railroads, the rivers were there, providing a way to travel, water gardens, wash clothes, and trade goods. With a river nearby you could catch fish, harvest berries, find good lumber from well-watered trees. In a territory thick with blackberry vines and old growth forests, the river was often the swiftest road.

It is singularly dreary here in Freeport. Grayer skies than I've ever seen back in Ireland, and that's saying something. Rain upon rain for days. But those green hills and this thick loamy soil are the raw materials for homesteading, and I'll be well on my way to my own farm soon.

John likes a woman who takes pride in what she does, this girl whom the land has made into a woman in only a few short years. Marilla hunts, fishes, boats, rides, shoots and guts the game, cooks, sews, makes soap and candles, sings in between. She can teach him a thing or two, and I bet she does. I bet that's half of how they fall in love.

It may have been men who initiated the move to Washington and Oregon territories, but it was the women who survived and enabled survival, passing on their genes to their children. Adapting and communicating, doing what must be done. Making homes where they found themselves. Embracing and loving the land, the trees and the rivers, the mud and the gray rainy skies. And maybe love isn't the right word, but love is what they did. The life force pressing on, lifting its head high, daring its children to survive despite being surrounded by death. And isn't that who humans really are, anyway? We know that death is inevitable, but in the meantime, we choose to live. It is a defiance of death to say that my children will outlive me, that my deeds and creations will survive after I am gone. And in many ways that is exactly what happened.

I like to think she kissed John first. One evening, fishing by the river. Mosquitoes thick as thieves, buzz droning in their ears. Blood pounding in their necks.

Then everything changes, and fast. But Marilla is used to that.

John has dark hair but green Irish eyes. A bit of a brogue that he's trying to hide, but when he's relaxed it slips out. A hearty laugh. He's his own man now, he's worked hard to get here, he's not afraid of hard work. He's in love with his work and the earth, with the muscle and sinew of it, with the new scars and toughened skin of it, the rich black soil by the river and the throbbing beat of its rise and fall, the slap of oars on the water.

There weren't many marriageable women around when John and Marilla met. But I like to think there was love involved because history doesn't say any different. It is just this: they married, they had children, then one day John died. Marilla remarried three more times but never had children with another man.

Truth be told, John's been baching it. Eating cold beans, barely baked potatoes from the coals, jerky and smoked fish. This beef stew at the Washburn's is the best thing he's eaten in a month of Sundays. And it's this warmth, the heat of the woodstove after the rain, the salt iron tang of broth on his tongue that's Marilla. She is meat, she is drink, she is hearth and iron and earth. And he's going to make this woman his wife.

When my grandmother was a child during the Great Depression, she raised and ate rabbits. I was horrified when I first learned this. Now I wish I had the guts to butcher a living thing the way she did. Some say it's not right to eat meat unless you kill it yourself, unless you can look into its eyes and tell it thank you. I know it's wrong but I eat store-bought rabbit anyway.

My grandmother gave my mother a white rabbit skin that she then gave to me. I used it as a rug for my Barbie dolls to play on. It is still the softest thing I have ever felt, except for the down on my newborn sister's scalp.

I have no children of my own. I am terrified to have something live come out of me. I am terrified of pain and of the stink of blood and of being a bad mother. I always felt guilty for not "taking care of" my baby dolls enough. Eventually I hardened myself and put them away.

I distinctly remember when this happened. I was six.

I already had a baby sister, and a brother was on the way. There were already more babies around than I could handle. Over the years I lived at home my mom would have four more.

Can you imagine giving birth to a full litter every month, like a female rabbit? Only to have your children disappear as soon as they grew up, carved apart to feed giants. But as the breeder they'd keep you alive, keep you around to get you knocked up all over again until one day you just couldn't do it anymore and then you, too, would die. Your skin a fur rug on some kid's dollhouse floor.

My great-great-great-grandmother raised ten children of her own. Married at 15, widowed thrice. She shot and killed her own game: bear, deer, pheasants. She made soap and clothes. Her portrait shows a formidable woman, solid as a hundred-year cedar, eyes piercing, hands and jaw set like river stone.

I shoot field arrows at an archery range and darn my own socks. That's as much like her as I'll get.

Have you ever seen a hundred-year cedar? The Cowlitz Valley used to be thick with them. When they were felled for lumber, swift-growing Douglas firs took over. Douglas firs were named by a Scotsman who was hired to catalog "newly discovered" species in the Pacific Northwest and ended up putting his name on nearly everything. Douglas firs like the sun, so they quickly take over clearings, reaching for the sky at the edges of things.

My first tree love was a Douglas fir in my mother's backyard on Douglas Street. Yes, really. This tree was so tall I could stand underneath it and not see the top. Its thick branches swayed and made swishing noises when the wind blew. In the summer, tangy sap bubbled out of the rough bark and stuck to my hands. Best of all, there was a sawed-off branch that stuck out like a microphone at just my child-size height. I would grab onto that tree and sing at the top of my lungs.

One particularly windy day, the sound of the blowing branches rose up to meet my voice and I fell silent, gazing upward, listening. I felt shivers spread through my body, a warm feeling, and tears came. It was the first time I had cried because something was so beautiful. It wasn't the last.

If I were to write the ending of my own story, after a good long life I'd die standing under a windblown tree. Lightning would strike and the tree would fall on me, killing me instantly at the height of my appreciative ecstasy. But nothing is ever that poetic in reality. Be realistic, a former boss used to say, as if his own preconceived notions were the only reality that could possibly exist. The term "reality" is so often misused this way, I've come to despise the word itself.

I'll probably have to settle for having my ashes buried at the foot of a tree. Mycelia can grow in and out of me and feed me to the forest. Maybe someone will eat me in a morel mushroom foraged and sold at a farmer's market, or in a pie made of blackberries plucked from the vine at the height of summer. I can be poetry if I like. Like energy or light, it goes on and on.

1854-1857: MARILLA

So at the river, the kiss:

We were laughing about something or other. I thought how perfect this night was, the sun going down over the low blue hills, the gulping splash of steelhead leaping in the river. The first bright stars of the Northern Cross shining down from the deep blue sky.

I leaned over and kissed John, right on the lips.

I don't know why I did it. It seemed right at the time. But afterwards he just looked at me dumbly like a fish hung up to dry and I thought I'd made a terrible mistake. Of course he wouldn't think of me like that. He'd seen the world, hadn't he? He'd been to New York and Rio, probably kissed lots of girls. He wanted to court a real woman, not an uncultured girl with mosquito bites on her arms. He didn't want me. I was merely a friend.

I didn't know what to say, and neither did he. I picked up my pole and my basket and left. "Marilla," he said, "come back." But I didn't want to talk about it. I walked home the long way so my tears would dry before I got there.

I didn't see John for a week. When he came over for supper, I found ways to keep myself busy. I excused myself early and went to my room to work on the darning.

But when Father called me to the table, I couldn't avoid John any longer. He sat there next to Father looking flustered, and I thought, it's my fault he can't look at me.

Father said he had given John permission to court me, if I wished to accept. I finally met John's eyes, and he blushed from nose to ears. All the bad feelings were gone, just like that.

Before he left, John gave me a bouquet of daisies tied with a bright blue ribbon. It was all too much to think about. My life was going to change in so many ways.

I put the daisies in a bowl of water next to my bed. Their white petals reflected the candlelight. I tied the ribbon around my wrist and blew the candle out.

I am no longer sad when it rains. Rain grows crops from seed, brings fish to the river, elevates trees. It also turns this road to muck and mire, slow going today as my horse chuffs and sweats.

I've left the farm and John for a few days to visit Mother and Father and my brothers in Olympia. I'm bringing my daughter Amanda with me. I haven't been up this way since I married John last year in my parents' new house. I would have preferred to be wed in the garden, but the rain kept us in. In our room under the eaves that night, we listened to the rain on the roof, our bodies blissfully warm under the covers.

Today, though, the weather is fair. Amanda and I crest the top of the hill and come out onto the high prairie. A field of tall grass and so many daisies it looks like snow. Snow, or a blanket of cottonwood fluff, or feathers from a seagull's down. Snow, or cool white stars, thick as milk on the plains. A golden smear of sun. The thick gray snags of old fir trees, spare and towering, sentinels of ancient days. Some might be older than Christ, older than the world, waiting for this very moment when the daisies bloom.

I untie the leather straps that secure Amanda's basket to the saddle and take her warm wriggling body into my arms. She arches backward, a caterpillar in calico, reaching for the sun. Wet lips searching, her toothless mouth full of gums. The horse grazes while I nurse, and as Amanda eats, so do I. A round of soda bread, torn into chunks. Hard cheese from the mercantile in Freeport. Cool water canteened at the stream.

Pink blossoms flash among the understory brush, heralds of future salmonberries. My mouth waters for fruit after this long winter. I peel the carrot in my bag, scraping orange radiance into the dirt. The horse lips up the shavings, swallows the carrot top whole.

The root is sweet, and soft from its long winter storage. The horse chuffs, frustrated at the meager quantity of his scraps. I pat his soft neck, pick the burrs from his mane. Scrape the mud from his hooves.

Amanda watches, her small eyes unfocused, listening attentively. She waves a tiny fist, her long fingers curled like new blossoms, and I give her a daisy to grip. She waves and crumples it as I tie her basket to the saddle, mount the horse and resume our trip. I sing to her as we go, wiping yellow pollen from her cheeks. She tears off petals, scattering them in our wake.

I was a child once, and I thought as a child. Now I have put those ways behind me, and more's the pity. Because when I see the wonder in my daughter's eyes, lighting up like candles at the sight of some new and glorious thing, I am reminded to be thankful myself. We are surrounded by the Creator's gifts every day. What I would give to see through the eyes of a child again, everything so fresh and lovely.

I think these things when there's time for my mind to wander. When I'm riding on these trips, or when I'm scrubbing clothes or peeling potatoes. The repetitive motions calm me and set my mind to order itself.

There is something about work that is the same as solitude. It pares me down to the solid quick, reveals the inner fortitude I do not know I have. A strength for which I am eternally grateful.

What strikes us most in this drive, are the magnificence of the timber on the mountain, and the roughness of the country for a highway. In this July weather it is well enough, jolting through the forest, over roots of giant trees, and into hollows between them; but, in the rainy season, it is a different undertaking....

Such a forest as this is something to remember having seen and fills completely our conception of solemn and stupendous grandeur. Fir and cedar are the principal trees. They stand thickly upon the ground, are as straight as Ionian columns, so high that it is an effort to look to the tops of them, and so large that their diameter corresponds admirably to their height. If there is anything in nature for which we have a love resembling love to human creatures, it is for a fine tree.

Frances Fuller Victor

The Bible says it's not good for man to be alone. Doesn't say the same for woman.

Besides, I'm not alone, out here with my horse under the white summer sky. The road from Freeport to Olympia is only two days' ride, and I'm bound to see a friendly face or two along the way. Not to mention the cedar trees alive with birds, fledgling crows squawking and robins singing their hearts out as if this summer were the last season on earth. For them, maybe it is.

But I feel confident that I have quite a few summers ahead of me, even in this new land where I once was sure I would die. It's only been four years, but I feel now as if I've always lived here. One foot in the forest and another in the river, with the trees, water, and clouds enclosing me like a great cathedral.

Sometimes it seems to me there is no end to this land, although I always arrive where I intend to go. The journey is not always easy, but neither is it too hard. By now, my horse knows the way better than I do, even along the road freshly churned to mud by a convoy of military wagons. Soldiers here in Washington Territory. Now isn't that a sight.

For what have we to do with distant wars? We are here, right now, surrounded by beauty. Green cedars, dark firs. Hemlock that curls its top like a lady curling her toes. Ravens, sparrows, and chickadees. The day moon, bright shell white in the slip of blue sky that flashes between the gray clouds and the deep green seam of the forest.

Good thing I left early and these June days are long. I can take my time. We have a few hours left to get to the halfway inn and shelter for the night. Already the sun lies low.

Tonight, after a supper of beans and hotcakes, I helped Mrs. Davis with the dishes before setting up my cot next to the woodstove for the night. Claquato is busy with all the travelers who stop here halfway between Fort Vancouver and Puget Sound. The trading post is open late so the men can smoke and play cards. Someone is playing harmonica, a tune I almost recognize. The musty smoke from the stove lingers in my hair. Beneath the woolen blanket I rub my hands to get them warm. It might be June but there is still a nip in the air, especially in the damp evenings here by the Chehalis marshland.

Amanda is swaddled comfortably in a box of blankets by my side. Somewhere a cow lows and cats brawl. I think of last night and John's arms around me in our own bed, and I let my exhaustion carry me into a deep and heavy sleep.

When Amanda was 5 months old, I put her into a basket, hung it to the horn of my saddle and went to Olympia to visit my parents. I rode to the Halfway House the first day, more than 50 miles. The next day I rode on to Olympia, getting there in time for supper. During the next few years, I made frequent trips on horseback to visit my parents.

Marilla Washburn

At my parents' house, we'll have fish for supper most nights. Other nights we'll have rabbit, which my younger brothers raise in hutches. Rabbits don't need much to thrive. Like the oysters my father seeds and harvests in Mud Bay, rabbits need only a little space and a little food to raise a family. I enjoy the salty kiss of oysters, especially when they're smoked.

I let my mother fuss over Amanda, giving me a respite from the constant chores of motherhood. I've missed my father and his quiet manner. He asks me of my life with John and nods approval. We sing as a family, too. John knows many good Irish tunes and seafaring songs from his journeys, but my parents know the old Quaker hymns by heart. Singing them brings me back to the clapboard church of my childhood back east, safe and surrounded by holiness.

This is the same way I feel riding through the countryside. I know what John Muir meant when he wrote of the great redwoods in California. These trees are my cathedral, the first wildflowers my incense. The rushing waters of the rivers and streams my Holy Spirit font. As Quakers we have always believed that His Spirit is everywhere. In my daughter's curled fists and dimpled smile, in my husband's equally dimpled smile and strong arms, an ever-present reminder that even this far west we are never alone. Only seeking companions, and as long as we seek, we shall find.

There, now—Amanda is crying to be fed, and my brother Walter wants my attention for this fat and shining fish he caught. The sun is sinking low over the lake, but the spring frogs are peeping in unison, bringing the first stars out with their shrill song.

Home again.

In the silver moonlight John opens his arms to me, and although I cannot see his face I can feel the warmth of his body. I lean into him, breathe in the scent of his sea-salt skin, and together we make love for lost time.

1865-1870: JOHN

We walk the rows of fresh-tilled earth, Amanda following in my footsteps, squinting in the light. After each step, I stop and dig a hole in the soil.

Amanda carries dried ears of corn from last year's harvest in her apron. "How many kernels go in?" I ask.

"Five," she says, plucking them from the cob. In her hand, they are yellow as the sun and shaped like teeth.

"Very good." I wipe the moisture off my forehead with my sleeve. "What else do we do?"

She cups the seeds and blows on them, infusing them with the breath of life. "There. Now they can grow."

"Good," I say. "That's just right."

She drops the kernels in each hole, patting the soil back over them. Together we plant the teeth of the sun.

The Cowlitz River was a source of wonder in my youth, a place where my sister and I walked the dogs and waded in the shallows, skipping smooth river stones. When heavy rains caused the river to rise and flood its banks, we stood at the edge and watched the gray water churn, the wind and rain chilling us through our plaid shirts down to the skin. In summer, the chirping of crickets and the buzz of motorcycles from the racetrack filled the air. When the comet Hale-Bopp arrived, we went to the river almost nightly for several weeks. The comet's paintbrush stroke of light made the stars look dim by comparison, even the brighter ones like my personal favorites, Deneb and Vega. At sixteen, I liked to stay up late to stargaze, strumming songs of unrequited love on my garage sale guitar.

John and Marilla farmed land and built a house on the Cowlitz River, not far from where I grew up. They traveled the river by boat long before the railroad or paved roads. The Cowlitz and Chehalis Indians traded along the river, bringing supplies to pioneer farms and trading salmon for butter, potatoes, and eggs.

The home that John built in the 1860s still stands. The two-story farmhouse faces a you-pick vegetable plot. Beyond that, there's a set of railroad tracks, and beyond those, you'll find the river.

When my mom and I visited the farm during a historic drought, sunflowers and cornstalks grew eight feet high, and the scent of rich river soil filled my nose. The closeness of the river and the pond must have kept the garden well-watered despite the heat.

I didn't remember how to pull the corn off the stalk, so Mom gave me a demonstration. After squeezing an ear to check for plump kernels, she grabbed the stalk above the ear and, with her other hand, twisted the corn down. It ripped off easily. Anthers and pollen shook loose from the tassels and dusted our hair as we waded through the close-planted rows.

Behind the house, a pond drew Canada geese to its cool waters. One ancient Douglas fir cast its long shadow over a picnic table, a reminder that this land used to be full of trees. John was a farmer first, but after the railroad was built he began to log his land and sell the trees, transporting them by train.

The nearby hills are still covered with evergreens, a sight I cherish. These trees are symbols of life. They've given people shelter and fuel for cooking and warmth. They've traded us oxygen for our carbon, held moisture in their branches and roots and returned it to the river, giving us more water to drink. They've helped their fellow plants, the river fish and the creatures of the forest, the people who have lived here since before the written word, and my ancestors and me. These trees and this river have worked together to give me life, and for that I am indebted.

Eat the salt, hold the woman, till the ground. Wipe the sweat from your neck and brow. Dip the bread, draw the water, dig the soil. Sing your horses as they pull the plow around.

Sow the seeds, dance the rain. Pray the earth and sun. Schuck the golden ears. Sweet the night when day is done.

There is security in soil. In crops and timber, in roots grown deep. In local mycelia. In river water and rain, layers of moisture to nurture the crops. Food and trees, shelter and fire. The air clean as God's whistle, cold as the blade of a hoe. If you are uprooted, it just means it's time to go, time to rebuild and replant. Live in a portable home, carry your children on your back. Keep on moving toward the promised land.

1871: MARILLA

The gun is loaded. This is an observation. It is also a metaphor. Perhaps it is a symbol. The loaded gun: American as apple pie.

The gun calls you by name. It sleeps under your pillow or your mattress. It whispers oiled secrets. It talks when you can't. The click, the slide, the bang.

It should be explained that Higgins, being an old-time gunman, had used the old-fashioned 44-caliber single-action frontier Colt, and affected the fashion prevalent among some men of sawing off the trigger and filing the notch down so that the hammer would not stay up. The gun was fired by throwing the muzzle into the air, catching the hammer with the thumb on the way up, and releasing it as it came down: a man who could do this could shoot faster than a man using a double-action gun.

Arthur T. Walden

I'm shooting targets with my brother Walter at the farm in Olympia. I can't believe he's almost a man. I suppose I am older, too.

He's showing off. He shaved the flintlock down on his pistol so he can toss it in the air and fire as soon as it comes back down. He's good, I guess. I still shoot better than him at a hundred yards.

He grins at me, shouts. "Beat that." I can barely hear him after the gun blast.

I spin the chamber, aim, and squeeze. There's a pop followed by a blast followed by an echo. The alder trees quiver.

Our ears ring as we walk across the pasture to examine the holes our bullets have left in the tree. We're mere inches apart, just the span of Walter's hand. But I'm still closest to the center.

Walter shakes his head. "You're a fine shot," he says.

I have to refrain from tousling his hair like I did when he was a toddler. I link my arm in his instead. "You'll best me one day," I say. He smiles as if he believes it.

Animals, like humans, come to rivers to drink. The eaters kill and eat. You could wait by the river at dawn to kill a deer, or so I imagine.

Bullets are expensive. It pays to be a good shot.

My ancestors had real things to fear. Death by starvation, cold, disease. The gun was a way to fend off one of these things. In the nineteenth-century Pacific Northwest, the gun was a useful tool. But even then, it was also a symbol of power and fear.

Fear of the unknown is more powerful today than it once was, precisely because we have become used to knowing so much. We have infinite knowledge available at our fingertips. One keyword in a search engine produces millions of results. The more we know, the more we fear what we don't know.

Or is it that we fear most what we know best?

My river is a long, muddy, burdensome thing, gray with sediment and gurgling like an old man with water on the lungs. It curdles down from the ashy mountains into the valley where my father's fields lie fallow.

I have come to the valley of the place in between. It is a wet, gray, rainy day, just like the days when we were rafting down the Columbia River, like all the winter days at Fort Vancouver. A sky that doesn't even pretend to be blue, clouds that hang like curtains all the way to earth, leaking onto everything.

I am always drenched. Or if not drenched, I'm damp. The water gets into my clothes, in my shoes and stockings, skirt and petticoat, bodice and sleeves. The neck and hem of my dress wick up rain and change their color.

I must move to stay warm. The wool blanket wrapped around me only does so much. My horse's withers steam as water runs off her mane. I have a little ways yet to go.

I am 87 years old and as I look back to my girlhood, I cannot help thinking how much more is done for the girls of today than was done for the girls of my day and generation. They have liberty that in our day was undreamed of. Sometimes, I wonder if the girl of today is as self-reliant, as self-sacrificing, as useful as girls were when I was a girl. I was married at 15, and was not only a good cook and housekeeper, but I knew how to take care of babies, from having cared for my brothers and sisters. I had ten babies of my own, and never had help. I could paddle my canoe on the river and handle the oars in a rowboat as well as an Indian. When my husband was away I could rustle the meat on which we lived, for I could handle a revolver or a rifle as well as most men. I have shot bears, deer and all sorts of smaller game. I used to take the revolver out and shoot the heads off grouse and pheasants. In fact, I became so expert with a revolver that at 50 to 100 feet I could beat most men.

During the early days, I lived in tents, in log pens and in log cabins. The modern mother would think twice before letting her 15-year-old daughter move out on a tract of timber miles away from any other settler, where she would have to kill the game for meat, cook over a fireplace, and take care of the children, make soap and make clothes for the children. In those days we could not run into some handy store to get supplies.

Marilla Washburn

West only makes sense on a flat earth, which is inaccurate. On our round earth, you can go west until you are east and then back west again.

Go far enough east, and you end up in the same place you would have if you had gone west.

1877-1896: WALTER

So here I am near the eastern edge of Washington Territory, past where the Columbia divides us from Oregon. Treeless expanses, blue fields of grain, crops abandoned by their planters as the war advances on these plains. If we had come to the edge of the world it would have been no different for the sheer magnitude of it all: these rocky cliffs that tumble into a sea of grass, purple sage drying into skeleton tumbleweeds, the ground sparkling with dew every morning.

If my desire was for home, I would have missed it by now. But I don't. I have no fondness for the salt-piss stink of oyster beds or the rotting algal mud of the bay. Nor do I miss the backbreaking work of hoe and plow just to produce a little food: potatoes here, corn there. Wheat and oats are a joke back home. Out here on the blue hills and plains they grow much better, with longer seasons of both sun and snow.

But my desire is for neither seas nor plains. What I want is trees, cool mountain streams, sharp pine tar scenting the air. When the army is done with me and I've earned my small coins, that's where I'll go.

Walter the gunslinger, the gold digger, the peacemaker. The first of Marilla's siblings to be born in Washington Territory. She was fifteen when he was born, and she would outlive him by more than 30 years.

The sun is a long slow throw of a silver dollar. Pvt. Walter Washburn hasn't slept all night. His army horse is all muscle and froth, pulling at the reins, headstrong, unlike his father's mild mares. This is the cavalry, in newly minted Washington Territory, on ancient Nez Perce lands.

He didn't sign up for this. Fifty men on horseback, fifty more on foot, the gray wash of the plains like filthy bath water. The silence is a sound he can hear in his spine.

Out of the blinding sun, the first arrows fall. Men and horses scream. Walter sights his rifle but there's no one he can see. The arrows come from everywhere and nowhere, all hunting for his chest, they'll seek him out like dogs and find a notch in his ribs or the nape of his neck or the tender meat of his thigh.

He fires a few rounds at the rim of the valley where the enemy must be hiding, but with nothing in sight, it's no use. He tells himself he's had a good life. He wishes he'd written to his Ma. The horse bucks and sidesteps the bodies of the men who've already been hit, the men with whom Walter has shared bed and bread, the men older and younger than himself.

They are curled around their wounds like children, clutching the wet red of their stomachs like women who know the time of their labor has come.

But not Walter, no, he is unhurt, he is on his horse clinging to life, reloading and firing, the stench of horse musk and spent gunpowder filling his nose, his eyes squinting along the vast blue horizon, burned by the unfamiliar sun.

Afterwards, the world rings in his ears. A hand on his shoulder. Men drag the bloated corpse of his horse away. He can walk. He is covered with blood but not wounded. It is the blood of the horse, after all, that draws the biting flies to him. They gorge like leeches.

He picks up his empty rifle. The battlefield is scored with bodies. He sees a few Nez Perce but more U.S. men, speared by feathered arrows. He thinks of flight, of prairie grouse rising in flocks. He is suddenly hungry, suddenly thirsty. He wants to plunge his face in that puddle of mud and drink it. He wants to go home. He wants to kill everybody who stands in his way.

Only he doesn't. He was here before, in his mother's womb. He knows this is not his land, not his people. The sky is so wide here it hurts.

They feed him whiskey and water, salt pork and gruel. When he is no longer hungry, he thinks. He thinks of trees and cold streams, mountains that pierce your heart with their peaks. He thinks he's lost his mind coming out here. Better that than lose his soul back home.

The thinking threatens to keep him awake, so he asks for another drink.

War was always here. It never left. It is in the river rocks and soil, the fields sown in blood. It is in the feather-fletched arrows, in the bird songs in the air. It follows the seep like uranium poison. It is in your bones and teeth and hair. Your horses drink war and your young men eat it.

If you kill off the young men, the older ones take their wives and raise children, perpetuating the violence in their genes. War is how the status quo remains, aching century after century with nothing changing except the shifting allegiances among those under the warmonger's bootheel. The wearer of the boot is the same.

I am American and I am embedded in this strange culture obsessed with liberty or death.

Somehow, guns have become the emblem of this false binary.

The yen to carry guns and threaten with them is often a response to existing fear but quickly becomes an exercise in power. Flexing muscles, bearing arms. And because we are human, it is inevitable that someone will pull the trigger at the wrong time, put a bullet in someone who didn't deserve to be treated like prey.

We are wasteful creatures, who kill and don't eat. We kill because we're trained to. Because we're told to. Because someone taught us to be afraid.

I walk east. I've made up my mind—this is the right thing to do. It is almost dawn when I approach the Nez Perce camp. I unfurl the white sheet I carry and hoist it above me like a flag.

I expect arrows. I expect death. I expect my last letter home will never be sent. I am never going back again.

The Nez Perce warriors come on horseback, bows and rifles drawn. I kneel in the good brown mud, holding out my white flag like an offering. I pray for mercy.

Against all logic, it's mercy I receive.

Having warned the Nez Perce of the next impending attack, I am put to work immediately. The whole world has narrowed to a single point: this lifting and hoisting, this work with my hands. Leather straps are tied, bridles and reins buckled. Children and the old are helped into wagons. Relentless, the night marches on.

I have no thought for tomorrow or even of my past. There is only now, a need for survival that consumes everyone's days. I am in no man's land here on the open plains, unable to hide, seen for what I am.

A city on a hill cannot be hidden. Neither can smoke.

As we flee, I find I have more time to think. I try to ignore the voice in the back of my head that tells me I am a coward. North through the mountains, so high up the snow still blankets the ground.

I'm wearing borrowed buckskin so as not to advertise my status as a deserting U.S. soldier. I burned the uniform in a campfire several nights ago. I can no longer smell my body in these skins. Instead I smell of musk and another man's sour sweat, woodsmoke and the gamey odor of deer.

The Nez Perce have shown me which roots are good to eat, some bark and the fruit of a tree that looks like tiny plums. Black salal berries, which taste better mixed with fat and dried. Red elderberries that go down better cooked. Red huckleberries, tart and eaten right off the bush. It wouldn't do to come down with scurvy. Man cannot live on meat alone.

As a thank-you, my companions have pledged to help me cross the border into British Canada. After that, I'll be on my own.

I saw depicted on that mountainside—
A picture in beauty grand,
Beyond the skill of mortal limner's hand.
I saw the different ages—
I saw the different stages.

James Meikle

It's peaceful here in the wilderness. Nothing but the trickle of mountain streams, occasional eagle screams for miles around. A man can really get a sense of his own heart beating, his own breath rising. His own thoughts, the purest torture that exists.

But no more of that. It's west I go, down toward the great Pacific, then north again to pan for gold on the banks of the Skeena River and find what I must do next.

When he first met Little Frogs, he'd been hungry for so long that he didn't even feel it anymore. Pine needle tea and the leather of his shoes were the only things that had kept him alive that winter.

When he saw her crouching by a clear, cold stream, he thought maybe he'd frozen to death and this was his final hallucinatory dream. He watched as she caught two fine salmon, cut them open, and speared them on sharpened cedar sticks to cook by a fire.

"Eat," she said eventually, when it became clear that Walter was too dumbstruck to speak.

The fish melted on his tongue like butter, its crispy skin crinkling against the roof of his mouth. The taste took him back to his childhood by the Sound, the saltwater inlets where he fished as a boy.

When he could speak again, he told her of the war he'd fled, of the bodies on the battlefield, of the secret shame of his fears. Why he couldn't go home, ever again. How he didn't sleep nights.

Somehow, she didn't walk away. Somehow, the stars appeared in the eastern sky, and even then they were still talking.

A stranger I was, and they gave me a place by the fire to sleep. They fed me venison and berries, gave me clean water to drink. I fell asleep surrounded by voices in a language I did not yet know, but I slept anyway. For the first time since I joined the army, I slept all night like the dead.

Trust thyself: every heart vibrates to that iron string.

Emerson

The smell of the sea sent my mind racing straight toward home. Olympia, on the southern banks of the Sound, the saltwater, algae, and rotting kelp stench of the muddy beds where my father's oysters grow. The docks where as a youth I watched the steamers come and go, carrying goods and people from Seattle, Victoria, and farther.

They say when you become a man you no longer care for your parents' opinions, but I don't think it's true. I think there is a part of you that cares long after they are dead and gone.

The Pacific Ocean: where rivers go to join the larger sea. The mass of holy water that joins the whole of the world together, that gave birth to life. The ocean that evaporates into rain clouds, quenching the planet's thirst from time immemorial. The ocean that Marilla longed to see and lived next to in her later years. The ocean that John crossed to find a new life. The ocean that filled the Sound and straits where Walter would sail between mother and duty and wife and gold. Yukon gold, for which men and dogs died side by side.

Circle City, Alaska was named by the miners who came there to harvest gold from the Yukon River. In 1895, they thought they had reached the Arctic Circle. (They were actually about 50 miles short.) A wooden sign that stands there today proclaims it's "The End of the Road."

For Walter, it was. In his early forties, alcoholism and rage finally took their toll. In 1897, he was killed in a barfight with a shot to the head. He was the one who started the fight.

A panoramic photo of Circle City, taken in 1899, shows a long line of buildings and cabins on the banks of the Yukon River. A canoe pulled onto shore. Two piebald dogs. Men standing, sitting, waiting. Three large signs advertising Pabst beer. And a boat dock labeled with a single destination: Victoria, some two thousand miles south.

Circle City quickly emptied out when the Klondike Gold Rush drew folks away in 1899. The population today hovers near one hundred. At the time of this writing, online photos show a brand new and completely empty hotel, a gas station, and a boarded-up Yukon Trading Post with various signs for "Café," "Bait," and "Beer." A broken-down Ford pickup and four kids on an ATV gone mudding by the river. There's a pioneer cemetery on private property with mostly wood-marked graves. I suppose Walter's bones lie there to this day, one neat bullet hole punched through his skull. All that gold picked out of his pockets, and the flask, too. It must have been a sight to see, all those men and dogs bearing witness to his death. Some no doubt glad to see him go. His common-law partner at the time, an Indigenous woman, might have breathed a sigh of relief. Maybe those were her descendants on the ATV.

The world gets smaller at the end of the road, you know. Narrows to a point. It's easy to see the past and the future here. All you have to do is blink.

After his mother's death and the births of his two children with Little Frogs, Walter left his family in British Columbia and followed the Gold Rush into the Yukon. No more causes, wars or gods, parents or wives, he was left to face his own drives and fears. Examine his own motives, or not. It was easier to change his name than change his ways. Easier to pass the days in work, the nights in whiskey.

Eventually, the days and nights ran together. Which tends to happen when you travel this far north.

West and east merely indicate the apparent motion of the sun and moon, which really only indicate the direction in which the world spins.

West is the opposite of the direction in which the world spins. West is the antimatter, the antagonist, the anarchist, the death-defier.

West is the direction of daring, of rugged individualism. A race against time. One last stand. Then, the inevitable.

Whiskey beer firewater what's the difference? Gold land status, all madness if you ask me. Wife mistress lady of the night, all the same where it counts. Don't make no never mind to me. Curse this head, this overthinking head that gets me into so much hot water. I wanna drown in a creek, let the cool mountain river swallow me down, fill my lungs and turn me to a fish so's I can swim out to sea and find another world. Worlds better than this one, let me tell you. I'm just a washed-up gold miner here at the end of the world fightin' all the other old fossils here over the last specks of gold dust we can suck out of the earth. If I was a cryin' man I'd be cryin' rivers, cryin' Mother, Mother can you hear me? I'm calling out to you from beyond your grave, I who have never heeded your counsel, to tell you that you were right, you were always right, I'm a fallen sinner in need of Christ's mercy and the closest thing I've found to it on this earth is in this saloon whore's embrace, she smells of perfume and pipe tobacco and if I can just rest my head upon her breast for a moment—just like this, girl, just for a moment, I just need a woman's touch—why I can imagine myself back home, with a wife and children who love me, in the days before I did them wrong. I can spirit myself back to the place where I was young, cradled in the arms of motherly love, her sweet salt and milk scent lulling me to sleep. Girl, you look a sight for sore eyes, let me buy you a drink. Whiskey, she says, whiskey, now that's my girl! Hah, you ain't scared of nothin, are you, you're a frontier woman now. Now mister, hey, back off a bit, don't you see I'm talkin to this pretty lady here. Oh no she's not, she's with me, aren't you sweet peach? Now listen here, I don't care for that kind of talk. And I'm not drunk, you jackass, I'm just a little—well now you've gone and done it—

[*unintelligible*] [*gun blast*] [*fade to black*]

Later, Higgins got into a row with Kronstadt, a bartender, and, sending him warning through his friends that he was going to kill him, appeared in the doorway of the saloon with his uplifted gun. Kronstadt instantly drew his gun from under the bar, and, instead of raising it, fired it from the level of the bar, striking his man under the eye, the bullet going out through the back of his head.

Arthur T. Walden

1896-1877: WALTER

The last thing I think when the bullet sears my flesh:
My family. I love my family.

I begin to travel back.

What I know standing here on the edge of the world is this: we might not have anything when we come into this life, nor can we take anything with us when we cross the rainbow bridge, but what we do have while we are here is abundance. Nothing is wasted, because everything and everyone serves a purpose.

In 2020, the Nez Perce nation reclaimed a portion of their ancestral lands, almost a century and a half after the Nez Perce war was fought in what is now eastern Washington State. I have lived in Washington State for all of my life, and I find it strange that I only learned about this war as a middle-aged adult.

Walter might have fought in this war, but then again, he might not have. Family history tells us that after his father passed away, he clashed with his new stepfather, then left home to join the army. At some point he went AWOL and fled to Canada, where he married a Gitxsan woman. When the Skeena River Rebellion took place, involving his sister- and brother-in-law, family records say he traveled to Victoria to secure a commission as a special constable in the Hazelton area where the Gitxsan lived.

Walter intended to protect his family while also earning money for his new position. However, more than two dozen constables returned with him, and one of them shot his brother-in-law in the back, killing him as he tried to run away.

Disappointed and angry, Walter eventually left his wife and two children and prospected for gold in Alaska. He was known as a sharpshooter. He was known to have a drinking problem. I think it's safe to assume he was both quick to anger and prone to fighting for a cause. An idealist with a temper, or an alcoholic who sensed the cards were stacked against him. Either, both. A personality is a continuum, not a dichotomy.

Measles killed many. Boarding schools took children away, changed them into people unlike their former selves. There was grief, loss. Talk of curses. On the other side, talk of cooperation with the foreigners, talk of progress.

Tensions and tempers, volcanic. A refusal of peace. Historic rebellion.

Two dozen plus white men, strangers but for one. Uniforms, boots, guns.

Kamalmuk flees, rightly fearing for his life.

Is this familiar?

Billy Green shoots him in the back. *The scoundrel was running away!*

The death of an(other) Indian.

The shooter, a "bully" who did a "rash thing"—one bad cop. And another. And another. And another. And another.

The years become centuries. And here we are. One murdered Indian. And another and another and another and another

I don't count myself religious anymore but I sure seen plenty of demons out here at night. Little Frogs was definitely not a demon, but she was also like nothing I'd ever seen before, neither god nor angel nor human nor creature, she was like a dream that you have without being asleep. Moving gracefully, always sure of her own power. The force of life that flowed through her was unmistakable.

Embarrassed by my filthy clothes and unwashed reek, I tried to thank her for the food. Water from upstream, berries from below, and slivers of salmon pulled off the skin as they roasted by the fire. I didn't know Salish well, yet, but the Chehalis people back home spoke something similar, so we managed to converse well enough.

The coals grew hotter as we fed the fire with dry twigs and cedar branches. Before I knew it the stars had come out.

I've done terrible things in this war, things I'd rather not talk about. I can't tell you anymore what I believe in.

There's a cave here in the cliffside with a fir tree growing in front of it. The tree is half as tall as me and crooked, like the constant winds have slowly bent the thing in half. I asked the tree how it got like that. It told me it's been fighting all its life.

If you're feeling sad, I want you to know it wasn't always this way. The stories of the elders tell us of long seasons of green things and flowers, of blue skies and stars glittering like mica on the walls of a cave. Our ancestors used to find their way by those stars, an atlas of celestial cartography.

Don't take too much thinking to figure out how to live right. Listen to your gut, and to the words your family raised you with. Thou shalt not kill. Seems plain to me.

Night here on the trail and I've been running for days. Not hard to follow these ruts, the ones that brought Mother and Father from Illinois. I wasn't even born yet. I guess that means I got more West in me than they ever will, which is why I ain't afraid.

Headed to British Canada where I can live free. Fir trees and rocky rivers, pure mountain streams. Wash all this dust off my soul.

The shadows fell as crepe on the water
Like splotches on a silver ribbon
As though to herald a sable night
The leaves on the branches of the trees
Whispered to the evening breeze,
"Where is thy unseen sea? Where is thy unseen sea?"

James Meikle

Out here past the Cascades, the world is exposed like the flat of a knife.

How different from the sea, and yet how much the same: the eye goes on for miles and miles, traveling past the place where one's feet could take them and alighting on some distant object, a ship, a prairie schooner, a tree. The fin of a killer whale or the hump of a buffalo. Gophers, or fish.

I'll admit I didn't pay much attention in church, but my parents taught me well. Do unto others what you would have them do unto you.

It is sometime later when the sky returns, blinding as a field of snow. The blood on my leg is thick and cold. Heat rolls down from the hills in waves. Flies cover the bloated belly of my horse, drinking saline from its clouded eyes. I am here in the valley of the shadow and somehow I have survived.

I am covered in my horse's blood. Dozens of men lie in the field around me, dying or already dead.

It's time for me to leave.

The so-called Civil War's already over and done. There's nothing left to fight for but this endless space out west, this place where I was born amid cholera and tears. The men around me are falling, struck by feathered arrows near their hearts. Those wounds will fester. They won't last long.

What a thing we've done here. We chose a beautiful place to die. I'm almost certain I've been hit and my leg is bleeding, maybe they can stitch me up or maybe they will amputate, either way there'll be plenty of whiskey but I won't live long enough to find out because my horse is going down. He's giving it his best but I feel the finality of his forelegs crashing beneath him, my leg pinned by his weight as he rolls over and breathes his last.

I, Walter Washburn, am out of bullets and bravery alike. I curl next to my fallen steed and shut my eyes. The battle rages all around me. I wait for the slow release of death.

They say you can't take it with you, but we took the rain with us straight across that rainbow sunset bridge and into sky country. Rain is a place, and you can carry places with you for as long as you like.

When we reached the top of the mountain, oh the sight! Columbia River, rushing down to the sea, stretching as far as the Willapa Hills. And floating on its surface the feathered seeds of cottonwoods, light as the bones of birds.

The sun is a ball of molten bullet slag, searing our eyes from the milk-white sky. I'm heavy on my horse's back, pressed between the earth and the sky. The world weighs me down.

We crest the hill and my heart sinks. There are so few of us, so many of them. Their arrows fly.

The clouds in this sky are as yellow as the dirt. His horse's hooves are covered with it. He is, too. They've both been sleeping in it and washing it off in the roiling Snake River where, before he was born, his elder brother drowned.

There was more here than met the eye, more to the stories and the land and the foamy brown river than anyone could presume to know. His father had taught him that. Learn from those who came before you. Learn from creation. Learn from the trees.

The trees were rare here, and spaced far apart, but where they grew on the riverbank they must have grown for a hundred years. Their trunks and limbs were that wide.

Walter wiped his face with a square of gray flannel. It came away yellow with dried flecks of mud. He slid the bullets into his gun. The oiled barrel clicked deep in its throat like a grandfather raven.

His horse made straight for the river, nostrils down, the scent of water in its mouth, the scent of going home.

1880: JOHN

Oh, sun just above the western hill,
Thy mystic, thy mild, thy wan-like light.
What beyond the visions home?
Thy dusky gloom, doth darken
A lighted dome.

Why unfold thy darkened veil?
What hideth thou from me
In some ocean crypt or ancient sea?

James Meikle

Something was wrong. I'd been walking out of the Freeport general store with my son, but all I could see was my birthplace, Cookstown, Ireland. I thought I'd left it behind me thirty-eight years ago. There was the Ardboe Cross, and the gray cobblestone streets. The air filled with Gaelic voices. Sewage followed the gutters down to the river, and my nostrils filled with the stench of burning coal and the yeasty warmth of rising bread.

Suddenly I was back home again, in the dusky cottage our family shared with the butcher's son and his noisy brood. My father sat drinking from the bottle at the kitchen table, his eyes red from whatever gut-rot was in his bloodstream now. His beard gone white.

He looked straight at me and said, "I'm dying, son."

With a shock, I saw it was true. An angry mass of intestines bulged out of his belly. I could see them shining wetly, smell the bile and blood.

Then I saw that I was exactly the same. Something had cut me open right across the middle, and the slick ropes of my bowels were slithering out. "Help me, Da!" I cried, beseeching him with outstretched hands, but it was too late. His head sank down upon his arm and the vision faded. I returned to my senses, and there in the bright spring sunlight my own son regarded me cautiously.

"It's alright, Father," he said, helping me into the wagon. "Let's get you home."

When had I grown so old?

I must have fallen asleep.
Was I dreaming I was on the mountain?

There was childhood; there was youth; there was age.
It was springtime; it was summer; it was autumn.
It was morning; it was noontime; it was evening.

James Meikle

I let them feed me blackberry root tea. I don't tell them I am dying. It will only trouble them.

My dear wife Marilla coaxes warm broth down my throat. This might be my last meal. We'll see.

Even now, I remember my first meal in America. A dry hunk of bread served with watery gravy on a tin plate, served to me through a slot in the door of my holding cell on Ellis Island.

It wasn't much worse than what they'd given us to eat on the ship, but it wasn't exactly what I had in mind for my first New York meal. I thanked God for it just the same. For all I knew, it could be the only meal I ate in America before they sent me back to England with my tail between my legs.

I cleaned up the gravy as best I could before setting the plate back down on the floor. As the sun set and exhaustion closed my eyes, I didn't even begrudge the resident mouse that skittered onto the plate with greedy paws. If there was room for me here, there was room for him, and in the land of plenty there would always be enough.

Thursday, June 3, 1880. Cilicia went to see her father.

Sunday, June 6, 1880. Rained some. Cilicia and I went to see Mr. Black. Stayed all night. Died easy.

Thomas Meikle's diary

He dips his bread in the sweat of his brow—eat, this is my body. He squeezes wine from the grapes on the vine—drink, this is my blood.

I watered this earth with my blood.

And as surely as the sun sets and rises every day, so have I loved this earth with an everlasting love and toiled over it with the sweat of my body. My tears have watered the parched earth, and my ashes have made the soil rich again.

Do they speak of fire in your holy book? Does it burn, maim, destroy? Or does it hover on the brows of the faithful like dove's tongues, gently flickering flames—the sun descending to anoint the sons of Adam once again, whose radiance grows wings.

1915–1928: MARILLA

I am here, finally, at the place where this rogue of a river meets the wide Pacific Ocean. I am reminded of the journey that brought my beloved John to me long ago, how he must have looked out from the deck of his ship to see these golden shores, the waves crashing on the rugged rocks, the solemn trees like watchtowers guarding the cliffs, the blue mouth of the estuary churning with seafoam and grit.

Orrin is a good and loving spouse, but there is no substitute for the husband of one's youth. What joy John and I took in each other's company, those long-ago days by the riverside! What plans we made, such far-fetched plans, that someday John would take me to see the ocean that I craved.

But it was not meant to be. Instead, we went straightaway to the happy labor of building a homestead, raising ten fine children, and harvesting lumber to sell from our land. How quickly those years flew by, and before I knew it the Lord had called him home.

Soon my time will come, too, and I will meet my John in that heavenly place. But today I am standing here, on the sandy breast of the sea. I gaze afar into its vast roaring heart. Salt spray clings to my hair and face, the seagulls call and play, and I think of my beloved sailing these spirited waters while my heart beats steadily on.

The songs we sang were mostly old. Some new, learned from the men baching it out on the trail. We'd stop for the night, build a fire, cook. The girls gathered buffalo chips and sagebrush for the fire. The women took up their frying pans and soon the camp was filled with the smoke of bacon frying, the scent of camp bread rising and molasses-sweetened beans. There'd be buffalo meat or antelope roasting, too.

That was seventy-four years ago when we crossed the plains, but even now when I close my eyes I can hear the songs we sang, smell the bacon and sagebrush popping, see the stars spread out like jewels to the very edges of the sky.

I had a dream last night of my beloved John. I dreamed of him as he was when he was young: with coffee-brown hair and bright green eyes, his work-roughened hands holding on to the railing of a ship. It was the ship he took from San Francisco to Astoria, the last large vessel he sailed on before he met me. The wind blew through his hair and the sun fell on his face, and I felt a deep piercing gladness in my chest to see him this way. "I've missed you so much," I said, but he couldn't hear me.

The next thing I knew, he was there in the water, floating calm and blue in the ocean. His eyes closed and his lips still.

Next to him was my brother Henry, his fourteen-year-old body perfectly preserved, as if nothing in the river that killed him nor the great wide sea could ever disturb his rest.

They floated together side by side like that, as the waves bore them west into the peaceful sea.

ACKNOWLEDGMENTS

First of all, gratitude: to my husband Tree, for tacos and pinball dates, snuggles and Star Trek, and always encouraging me. To my parents, siblings, and extended family—you are the reason this book exists. To my Artist's Way co-conspirators: for skydiving, stargazing, listening to the first scene I wrote for this book, and never letting me get in my own way—thank you. To Eliza Tudor, whose collage and kintsugi workshop at BARN showed me a path forward for *The River People*. Much gratefulness to The Lovelies, for believing in this book during my moments of doubt and listening to me ramble about it *ad nauseam*. And thanks to Summer and the rest of the amazing crew at Unsolicited Press. I'm honored to work with you.

This is a hybrid work. There are historical quotes from real people, and bits of nonfiction and memoir woven in with poetry and historical fiction. (Any factual errors are mine.) Small portions of this book were previously published in different forms in "Refugia" (The Pitkin Review), "The Enduring Green" (Gaia Lit), "What a River Needs" (Catamaran), and "Photosynthesis" (Poetry on Buses).

In real life, I am Marilla's third-great-granddaughter. In the spirit of getting at the emotional truth behind these stories, I have taken creative liberties with this fictionalized account of my ancestors' lives. What is fact: Against her will, Marilla Washburn traveled the Oregon Trail with her parents and siblings. In her teens, she met and married John Black, eventually giving birth to ten children. One of them was Cilicia, who married Thomas Meikle and became my great-great-grandmother. The poems in this collection are from their son, James (1880-1951). Their son Walter Meikle (1883-1971) is also quoted in this book.

The Meikle poems and quotes are from historical family documents collected in my great-aunt Grace Collins' self-published book, *Ever Onward*. They are reprinted by permission of Grace's children, Becky, Paul, and Kathy. Grace's tireless research over thirty years supplied the histories of Marilla, John, and Walter that inspired me to write this book, and for that I will be forever grateful.

I didn't change much of Marilla's story, but I made a few educated guesses as to the places and people she might have encountered. These include the Davis family in Claquato and African-American pioneer George Bush and family, who famously shared their home and their food with folks traveling through the region. The source material for Marilla's narrative and her quotes comes from her interview with Fred Lockley published in the *Oregon Journal* in 1926.

I have faithfully followed John Black's journey from Ireland to Oregon, although I've had to fill in some of the details with information from historical records of the time. He was indeed fleeing an alcoholic, abusive father, and changed his name so he could embark on not one but two dangerous ocean crossings.

More facts: Marilla's younger brother Burzilla Washburn changed his name to Walter later in life. After his father's death, his mother remarried and he joined the army. He deserted his post and fled to what is now British Columbia, marrying a First Nations woman named Lucy ("Small-frogs") Genkum-na-ye. Family records informed what I wrote about his role in the Skeena River Rebellion and his departure from his family to prospect for Yukon gold. His involvement in the Nez Perce war and collaboration with the Nez Perce are fictional, however—my own interpretation of Walter as a troubled idealist. His death by gunfire in an Alaskan bar is true.

It isn't easy to tell the stories of one's ancestors. I wanted to honor them properly by recognizing their love and courage, and by having compassion for the tough situations they endured. However, they're also human, and they were subject to the biases of their times. Encouraged by the U.S. government, they moved onto land that wasn't theirs, potentially displacing people who already lived there. Between Walter's military service and his gunslinging years, he might have killed innocent people. Today I have easy access to shelter and food, in part because I've benefited from my ancestors' actions. I have done my best to acknowledge this moral ambiguity and to still honor what was good in my ancestors' lives. May we learn from our history and make better choices for our future.

SOURCES

Bowles, Samuel. "Letter XIX. Through Washington Territory." *Across the Continent: A Summer's Journey to the Rocky Mountains, the Mormons, and the Pacific States, with Speaker Colfax.* Samuel Bowles & Company, 1866.

Collins, Grace. *Ever Onward.* Gorham Printing, 2012.

Lockley, Fred. "Marilla R. Washburn Bailey." *Oregon Journal.* March 3 & 4, 1926.

Victor, Frances Fuller. *All Over Oregon and Washington.* 1872.

Walden, Arthur T. *A Dog Puncher on the Yukon.* 1928.

ABOUT THE AUTHOR

Liz Kellebrew writes poetry, short fiction, and essays from the Pacific Northwest. She wrote her debut poetry book, Water Signs (Unsolicited Press), while riding the ferry between Seattle and Bainbridge Island. Her poems have appeared in public art installations and literary journals such as About Place, Room, and Writers Resist. She received The Miracle Monocle Award for Innovative Writing, and her fiction has been shortlisted for the Calvino Prize. It also appears in various anthologies and journals, including The Conium Review, The Coachella Review, and Unreal Magazine. A member of the Academy of American Poets, she holds an MFA in Creative Writing from Goddard College. Learn more at lizkellebrew.com.

ABOUT THE PRESS

Unsolicited Press is based out of Portland, Oregon and focuses on the works of the unsung and underrepresented. As a womxn-owned, all-volunteer small publisher that doesn't worry about profits as much as championing exceptional literature, we have the privilege of partnering with authors skirting the fringes of the lit world. We've worked with emerging and award-winning authors such as Shann Ray, Amy Shimshon-Santo, Brook Bhagat, Kris Amos, and John W. Bateman.

Learn more at unsolicitedpress.com. Find us on twitter and instagram.